THE ELK OF AMOR

Betsy Kurth Quinn

*Norma –
I hope you
enjoy my book!
I love you! Love,
Betsy*

Illustrations by
Donna Atkinson

Willow Glen Publications

Library of Congress Catalog Number: 2020920655
ISBN: 978-0-9998090-2-0

For my husband, Michael,
And our sons and daughter-in-law,
Taylor and Sarah, William, and Patrick

"Love does not delight in evil but rejoices with the truth. It always protects, always trusts, always hopes, always perseveres."

CONTENTS

The sun warmed Georgia's back. She was small for her age—though eight years old, she was often mistaken to be only five or six. After zipping up her sweatshirt and tightening her shoelaces, Georgia skipped down the sidewalk past the mailman. She smiled because today was Saturday, her play day! The autumn chill blanketed the ground with colorful leaves of gold, crimson, and rust. A gust of wind rustled the tree branches, showering a cascade of leaves upon Georgia. She snatched a shiny red maple leaf from the ground and began her game, tossing it high into the air and then chasing it to its landing spot. The wind blew again sending her leaf swiftly skyward. Just as quickly, she ran past the grocery store and repair shop in pursuit. She didn't want to lose her little leaf as it sailed gaily aloft.

Suddenly, the wind stopped whistling and her leaf fluttered down. Georgia raced to the landing site. To her amazement, the leaf teetered on top of an antler and fell to the ground. Forgetting her leaf, Georgia was struck by the massive monument that suddenly stood before her: a bronze elk shining majestically in the sunlight! At the bottom of the statue was an inscription that read 'AMOR VINCIT OMNIA.' "He's beautiful. I'll ride him," she exclaimed. Georgia scrambled up onto the elk's hind legs and over its tail. Scooting upon its back, she dusted dirt and cobwebs off its antlers and face. She soaked in the radiating warmth of the elk, and her eyes grew heavy as she yawned. With a big stretch she hugged the elk's thick neck and slowly closed her eyes.

A sudden jolt awoke Georgia. She instinctively gripped the Elk's neck so as to not fall off. At first she thought a storm had kicked up because of the intense wind, but the clouds above her looked calm, wispy and white. Big grey clouds were visible on the horizon, though they appeared to be quickly approaching. Or, was she quickly approaching them? Georgia realized that she was soaring off the ground, each second climbing higher in the sky. When she gazed downward she could see the whole town. Then, in her amazement, she saw her own house. Her father was raking the leaves in the back-yard and she called out to him, "Hey, Dad," but he couldn't hear her.

Her excitement quickly turned to fear. After all, she didn't know where she was going or when or if she would ever return. The Elk soared higher and higher through the clouds. Georgia shivered; the wind whipped around her body and tossed her ponytail around like a kite's tail. The ride became more bumpy, and Georgia instinctively tightened her clasp around the Elk's neck as they passed through a rain cloud. The turbulence caused Georgia to bump her head against the Elk's neck. In the next moment, the Elk gently landed in a thick wooded forest.

The Forest

Georgia gazed at her new surroundings and tried to figure out what she was doing in such a peculiar land. She surveyed the landscape and heard rushing, gurgling water. The Elk walked towards a stream and bowed down to allow Georgia to get off and take a drink. Realizing how thirsty she was, she scampered off the Elk's back and bent down to gulp handfuls of cool water. It tasted as sweet as honey but now hunger pains stabbed at her belly.

The Elk slowly began walking away from her, but before he got too far, she scurried over to his side and walked close beside him. They came to a clearing surrounded by tiny fir trees. In the center was a large white banquet table overflowing with food.

The Elk stopped at the entrance as Georgia ran to the table, and began to devour the food, filling herself with fruit, cheese and fresh warm bread. The apples were crisp and juicy, the grapes burst an explosion of tangy juice in her mouth, the tart cherries tingled her tongue and the pineapple dripped sweet juices down her chin.

After eating her fill she walked over to the Elk as he stood staunchly gazing at her. Georgia returned his look. An unusual quiet hung in the fresh forest air—no birds were chirping, no squirrels rustling leaves. The silence made her feel uneasy, as if she and the Elk were totally alone. "But how did this food get here and who prepared this banquet?" she asked the Elk. As she looked back at the banquet table it vanished before her eyes. Confused and tired after a long flight and a hearty meal, she said nothing. Just as silently, the Elk guided her to a canopy of low trees. Pawing the ground, he nestled a tiny bed of leaves and soft moss. He lay down and Georgia curled up beside him and rested her head on his back. She slept a wonderful sleep.

When she awoke, she found the Elk guarding her patiently. He bowed down as a signal for Georgia to ride on his back again. As the Elk walked, the trees separated and a cobblestone street lay beneath them. In the distance Georgia could see a grey stone fortress with menacing towers. As they drew closer to the entrance of the fortress Georgia heard strange noises. She leaned in to ask the Elk what was happening when something amazing caught her eye. In front of her stood two sheep dressed in military uniforms. With scowling faces they stood guard. But, as Georgia and the Elk approached, they dropped their swords in fear and bowed their heads to the Elk. The sheep then pulled on a lever and the gate opened with a thunderous clash.

9

The Fortress

I nside the fortress were all kinds of forest animals: bears, tigers, lions, rabbits, squirrels, chipmunks, songbirds, groundhogs, ducks, owls and so many others. The animals bickered: crows fussed at roaring lions, bears growled at chipping chipmunks, ducks quacked furiously at fighting rabbits—overall, a wild mess! The stronger animals busily built the fortress while the smaller animals searched for supplies. All of the animals were too occupied to notice Georgia and the Elk walking into the courtyard.

The Elk stood up on his hind legs, lifting Georgia high into the air. Steam snorted out of his nostrils and he stomped his hooves violently, making the ground quake and the fortress shake. All of the animals abruptly stopped what they were doing and shuddered in fear at the sound and sight of the Elk.

The Elk then raised his right hoof as a sign for silence, and after a moment nodded to the biggest bear. The bear cleared his throat with a low growl, and then started to speak! "As the oldest member of our community, I have seen many changes occur in this forest kingdom, but what has recently happened is the worst yet. Oh, Great Elk, we, the animals of the forest, are in bondage. Three nights ago, while all of us lay sleeping in our dens, the Evil Oinkler's followers captured us and brought us here to repair his dwelling. He makes us work day and night and hardly gives us enough food to eat. Our children are starving. We have all become enemies and we can't stop quarreling. We're sick and tired, please rescue us from our troubles!"

Georgia and all the animals waited for the Elk's response. Georgia sat blinking, unable to comprehend her surroundings. All was quiet. The Elk snorted and then spoke. "Dear brothers and sisters, this news you tell me saddens my heart. I am deeply sorry for the tormenting you have received. However, the quarreling among you must stop before you can conquer the Oinkler. You must love one another, and stop fighting immediately."

At this, the animals murmured and eyed each other suspiciously. Again the Elk raised his hoof, and, when it was silent, began to tell a story. "I once knew two squirrels. They were inseparable friends. One day, they decided to build a storehouse to share during the winter. They began to build it but the weaker of them grew very tired. After a while, he quit helping build the storehouse, and instead tried to do his part by gathering berries and nuts to put in the storehouse. The other squirrel grew jealous and felt cheated because he thought he was doing all the work. Then, the weaker squirrel became angry and they both began yelling at each other and got into a big fight. Eventually, they realized that they were both working toward the same goal but in different ways. After apologizing to one another, they went back to their respective tasks. Now, who do you think was right for being angry, the strong squirrel or the weak squirrel?"

Georgia and the animals pondered the Elk's question and then Georgia spoke up, "Neither squirrel should have been angry. They were both doing what they could to help each other. The strong squirrel was able to build the storehouse and the weak squirrel was able to gather nuts and berries to put in the storehouse."

"You are correct, Georgia," replied the Elk. "Friends should love one another and seek to remain friends. Therefore, you animals, although you are tired and hungry, you must stop arguing. Arguing will not help you to escape the Oinkler's tyranny. Please apologize to one another because we must all work together. Where is the evildoer now?"

The meekest member of the forest spoke up, "I, Mr. Mouse, overheard the Oinkler speaking to his minions. He mentioned that he was going to other lands to create more violence, destruction and hate among their citizens. I believe he's supposed to return shortly."

"Well, then we haven't much time," replied the Elk.

"We must work fast," said Georgia.

The Elk began breaking the bonds that bound the prisoners by crushing the chains with his sharp hooves. After he freed all of the animals, he let them leave the fortress. They immediately apologized to one another—and much affection ensued, with bear hugs and nose nuzzles, merry chirps and excited tail-wagging. Georgia sent them back into the woods to find food and rest. Georgia noticed the Elk scratching in the dirt. He wrote down instructions for the forest animals: LOVE CONQUERS ALL. After he finished writing, he said, "Come along Georgia, our work is finished here." Confused, she hopped on his back. He took off through the woods.

Georgia pondered, "I don't understand, I thought we were going to help them defeat the Oinkler."

"We have, my young one, we have. They don't need our help anymore," replied the Elk.

"But, how will showing the Oinkler love conquer him? It doesn't make sense," Georgia said.

"You will see, my friend, you will see." The Elk stopped talking and galloped faster and faster. The trees blurred into hazy green masses.

The Ocean

Once through the dark forest, they came to the shores of an ominous ocean with huge crashing waves and frothy foam. Instead of stopping on the beach, the Elk suddenly leapt into the water and dove down, down, down, deep into the dark blue depths! Georgia gulped, held her breath and closed her eyes as soon as she felt the cold water. She was afraid she would drown if she opened her mouth.

Quickly out of breath, she gasped for air and realized that she could breathe! "But, how? I am in the water, right?" Slowly opening her eyes, she focused her gaze on beautiful sea creatures: spiny urchins, octopuses, multi-colored fish, dolphins, whales and sharks. Breathing water made her feel even colder than flying through the sky, compelling her to hug the Elk even tighter.

Georgia could sense something was amiss. Landing in a sea cave illuminated with bright pink coral, the Elk and Georgia waited for the sea animals to gather around. As they gathered close, Georgia did not notice any baby sea creatures. "This is not right, where are the young ones?" Georgia asked.

The great blue whale bellowed, "A great calamity has overcome us and we are powerless." Then he began to cry, but instead of teardrops falling from his eyes, big sad tear-bubbles poured out and floated up to the ocean's surface.

Georgia pushed off of the Elk's back, swam over and patted the whale on his cheek. "Please tell us, we want to help," she urged.

"Thank you, I am sorry that I cried. Yesterday, when all our little fish were in school, the evil Oinkler spread a poison throughout the school and now our children are sick and close to death. We don't want them to die," the whale said with a sob.

"That's terrible!" exclaimed Georgia.

"Yes it is," cried a mother starfish. "We have given up all hope, we can't do a thing," replied a sea urchin. "The Oinkler told us that until we bow down and worship him, our children will remain sick," a great white shark tearfully sniffed. "Each hour our babies' gills grow weaker and weaker, there's no hope left," squeaked a seahorse.

The Elk replied, "Dear brothers and sisters of the sea, this news you share grieves me. I am deeply sorry for this awful plague that has fallen on your community. First, you must resist your discouragement and doubt before you can conquer the Oinkler." At this, many sea creatures sobbed louder and buried their heads in their fins, but the Elk calmly raised his hoof and said, "Let me tell you a story.

"Once upon a time, two sea crabs lived on the ocean floor. They were brothers and they loved their family very much. One day, while they were playing outside their shell-house, a great storm came along, tossing the sea and shifting the ocean floor. The motion caused the crabs' shell-house to crash upside down and trapped their parents inside. Well, one tried with all his might, digging through the sand to save his parents while his brother ran away crying in despair. Miraculously, the tide shifted directions and lifted the shell just enough that the crab was able to squeeze under the shell, find his parents and save them.

"Now, which brother was wiser, the one who had faith or the one who gave up?" asked the Elk.

"The one who had faith!" exclaimed Georgia.

"Correct," said the Elk. "You sea animals must have faith. All of you are like the crab who ran away in discouragement and despair. Don't be discouraged! You should be like the brother who had faith," he stated.

"We won't give up, we know that you can heal our children!" exclaimed the eel. "Please have mercy on us, the fish of the sea. Please help us overcome the Oinkler," replied the sea animals. "Oh, Great Elk, please save the children and teach the animals how to stay safe from the evil one," pleaded Georgia.

The Elk spoke to the animals of the sea, "Because of your

strong faith, your children will recover. Go and tend to their needs. Then, I will give you instructions to save you from the Oinkler." Georgia dismissed the sea creatures while the Elk began pawing a message deep into the sandy sea floor. The message was as Georgia guessed, LOVE CONQUERS ALL. "Come along Georgia," replied the Elk in a serious tone.

"I know, I know. We're finished here," she said with a big shrug, shaking her head and looking to the ocean surface. Then, she climbed upon the Elk's back and with lightning speed, they rose to the surface of the ocean and were on the sandy beach within minutes.

The Beach

Georgia's damp clothes dried quickly from the heat of the sun. It was afternoon and all the clouds had vanished. She hopped down off the Elk and began skipping around while humming a tune: "Amor Vincit Omnia, Amor Vincit Omnia..." Repeating the inscription that she read at the base of the Elk earlier in the morning. "Amor Vincit Omnia..., Amor Vincit Omnia...," she hummed as she gaily ran along the shore kicking seashells.

Several hours passed as she played in the sand. She was having so much fun that she didn't notice how low the sun had dropped. She then looked for the Elk, but he was gone. In fright, Georgia ran up the beach following a trail of hoof prints. To her relief, she found him picking up driftwood pieces with his mouth to build a fire as the sun set over the ocean.

As the fire crackled, the Elk lay down and beckoned to her, "Come here my child and rest awhile." Georgia nestled between the fire and the Elk as her gaze transfixed on the dancing orange flames. The Elk's low soft voice broke the silence. "You see my child, I will not always be around. Do you understand? You are a brave little girl. You have seen many things. Everything from today may seem strange and unreal. But, someday, I hope you will understand what has happened.

"You see, everything has a purpose. You have a purpose. I know that some people make you feel worthless. They might say you are too young or too little. But remember this: No one is ever too young to know the truth you've learned today. I hope you remember the lessons that you have learned and that you will teach them to others. Remember how we found the animals in the forest arguing with one another, and how the sea animals were without faith? Do you remember what saved them from the evil Oinkler?"

Georgia looked up into the Elk's big glimmering eyes. "Yes. I know. Each time, love conquered the Oinkler. But what will happen to the animals now?" she asked.

"I will show you," the Elk said. Georgia hopped on his back and rode to the forest's edge. Peering through the trees, she saw all of the forest animals, content and cheerful, feasting together as one loving family. Georgia sensed that they were now safe from the Oinkler. As they flew past the Oinkler's fortress they saw him sitting in the middle of his courtyard in a puddle of mud with snot dripping down his snout. His beady eyes glared at the Elk and through his greenish brown teeth he shouted angry words but remained sitting lazily, alone and complacent in his own misery. Then, Georgia and the Elk journeyed to the ocean shore and she peered through the wavy tide. She could see the families gathered around a table giving thanks for their health and happiness. Georgia knew in her heart that they, too, were safe from the Oinkler's threats. "As you have just seen, the animals' great love and faith in one another has caused the Oinkler to flee from their presence. He has no compulsion to bother those who don't hate one another. He detests love and, therefore, avoids love. Their unselfish love has turned away their strongest foe. Remember this truth that you witnessed today: Love Does Conquer All!" exclaimed the Elk.

Home

As Georgia pondered his words, he interrupted her thoughts, saying, "It's getting late. Climb upon my back and I will take you home now."

Tears filled Georgia's eyes. "But, I don't want you to leave me. I want to stay with you," she sobbed. Big wet tears streamed down her cheeks.

"You can't come with me right now. Some day you will. Besides, I will never really leave you. I will always watch over you and protect you. You just won't see me," replied the Elk. With her eyes blurry, Georgia held tightly to the Elk's antlers as they galloped home. With a jolt, Georgia looked around, realizing the sun had set and the wind was howling. The forest, fortress, and ocean were nowhere to be seen. The Elk's bronze neck had grown cold and stiff.

Georgia recognized, "I've returned to the park!" She slid

down off of the statue and began walking home. She wondered if she had had a dream. "What did it all mean? What did 'Amor Vincit Omnia' mean?" As she walked up the front steps to her house, she reached into her pocket. She felt something round and cold and pulled it out to look at it. In her hand lay a bronze medallion with an Elk embossed on the front and the phrase 'AMOR VINCIT OMNIA' engraved around the elk. Turning the medallion over, Georgia saw the words 'LOVE CONQUERS ALL.' "It wasn't a dream!" she said, as she walked inside her house.

THE END

ABOUT THE AUTHOR

Betsy Quinn

Betsy is the founder of Willow Glen Publications. Betsy graduated from James Madison University with a Bachelor of Arts in English. She was the primary force that transformed her great-grandmother's rough manuscript into Willow Glen's first book, *Gold Rush Girl: Pioneer Life in the Black Hills*, a memoir about her early life spent in the Black Hills of the Dakota Territory in the late 1800's. Betsy lives in Oak Hill, Virginia with her husband Michael, and is a mother to three adult children.

ABOUT THE ILLUSTRATOR

Donna Atkinson

Donna graduated from the Ontario College of Art and Design (OCAD) with honors in Fine Art and spent a year abroad in Florence, Italy where she studied at the British Institute. She has shown her work in both Toronto and Virginia (where she now resides) and has work featured in numerous private collections which include The Toronto Star and The Williamsburg Foundation. Her illustrations have been featured in *Saturday Night Magazine*, *Newsweek*, *Virginia Commonwealth Magazine*, *The Virginian Pilot*, and *Ledger Star*.

CPSIA information can be obtained
at www.ICGtesting.com
Printed in the USA
LVHW072032010521
686220LV00002B/7